Rubber Duck

Finds Christmas

11/3/2013

Rhodora M. Fitzgerald

Rubber Duck Finds Christmas

Rhodora M. Fitzgerald

Copyright 2013 by Rhodora M. Fitzgerald

ISBN-13:978-1492980063

Rubber Duck opened his eyes and peeked over the edge of the fuzzy cotton ribbing that tightly hugged his body. His eyes grew wide when he discovered he had been stuck in the top of a sock. From where the sock hung at the top of the fireplace mantel, the floor was a long way down.

"How did I get here?" Rubber Duck wondered.

It was barely daybreak, when the room suddenly came alive with four loud, bouncy children. Sleepy parents watched as their children joyfully ripped open every package under the brightly lit tree. Rubber Duck cringed and sank deep inside the sock when the children suddenly remembered their Christmas stockings and charged the fireplace all at the same time.

Once each stocking had been emptied and tossed aside, the children settled down and quietly played with their new toys. Rubber Duck, who was forgotten amongst the excitement, decided to hide beneath a pile of wrapping paper. Little did he know he would soon be scooped up along with the papers and ribbons. When the box of papers landed on the back porch, Rubber Duck bounced out and landed head first in a pile of cold, white fluff.

"Brrrr," shivered Rubber Duck. "It's cold out here."

Rubber Duck didn't know what was happening. His new home was full of noise and confusion. The only thing he did know was he wanted to get far away from it all. Rubber Duck spotted a river nearby and decided to go for a swim, but when he arrived at the river he was sad to find it was frozen. While he sat pouting on the snowy river bank, a furry little rabbit skidded by on the frozen water.

"Woohoo!" yelled the furry little rabbit, when he spun out of control and slammed into the river bank.

"Whoa!" Rubber Duck jumped back. "Are you okay?" he asked.

"Of course I'm okay," the furry little rabbit giggled.

"What are you doing?" Rubber Duck asked.

"I'm having a ride on God's super slide," said the furry little rabbit.

"Oh," Rubber Duck sulked.

"Why are you so sad?" the furry little rabbit asked.

"I wanted to swim," said Rubber Duck. "But the river is frozen."

"Well, since you can't swim, you should come and slide with me," suggested the furry little rabbit, while he spun a circle on the ice.

"Well, okay," said Rubber Duck. "It does look like fun."

So, the new friends slipped and slid a far ways down the river. They hollered and giggled when they bumped into each other. The furry little rabbit made a snowball and packed it tight. Then he slid it across the ice to Rubber Duck. Rubber Duck used his tail to swish it back. The furry little rabbit swatted it back with his paw, and a game of ice hockey was born. Back and forth, down the ice they went passing the snowball to each other. Rubber Duck and the furry little rabbit were having a great time, but it wasn't long before the day grew into night. When they finally looked up to the river's edge, they discovered the river had led them into a small town.

The streets were mostly quiet. Only a few people still dashed from house to house while they celebrated the spirit of Christmas. Although the stores were closed, their fronts were still decorated with colorfully wrapped presents, and festive decorations framed every window in town. Twinkling lights of red, blue, yellow and green brought many homes to life, and in the front window of nearly every house was a decorated tree wearing the same beautiful lights.

"Wow," said Rubber Duck.

"Pretty amazing, isn't it?" asked the furry little rabbit.

"Yeah," said Rubber Duck, his jaw still gaping.

"Careful," said the furry little rabbit. "Stay close to the buildings so you don't get stepped on."

"Why is everyone in such a hurry?" asked Rubber Duck.

"People are always in a hurry," said the furry little rabbit, "especially during the holidays."

"Why is everything so sparkly?" asked Rubber Duck.

"It's Christmas," said the furry little rabbit.

"Christmas?" Rubber Duck tipped his head to the side. "What's that?"

The furry little rabbit tipped his head like Rubber Duck. "Christmas," he said again. "Don't tell me you've never heard of Christmas?"

"Sorry," said Rubber Duck. "I don't know what Christmas is."

"Christmas is the day baby Jesus was born," said the furry little rabbit.

"It looks like a big deal," said Rubber Duck.

"It is a big deal!" said the furry little rabbit. "Christians everywhere celebrate the birth of Jesus. Once you know who Jesus is, you can't look at all the twinkling lights and decorations and not see Jesus."

Rubber Duck glanced around. "I don't see Jesus," he said.

"Jesus is everywhere," said the furry little rabbit. "And not just in the decorations, lights and presents."

"Who is Jesus?" Rubber Duck asked.

"Jesus is the Son of God," the furry little rabbit explained.

"God has a son?" asked Rubber Duck.

"Uh-huh," the furry little rabbit nodded. "God sent Jesus to teach us the way He wants us to live."

"I want to see Jesus," Rubber Duck decided.

The furry little rabbit thought for a moment. "Follow me," he said, and he bounded off across the street.

When the furry little rabbit finally stopped in front of a church, he pointed. "There! That's the baby Jesus," he said.

Rubber Duck hurried to catch up with the furry little rabbit. "In the hay?" he asked.

"Uh-huh," said the furry little rabbit.

"He's not moving," said Rubber Duck. "Is he okay?"

"Well, that's not the *real* baby Jesus," said the furry little rabbit. "This is just a model."

"Oh," said Rubber Duck. "Where's the real Jesus?"

The furry little rabbit thought for a moment. He wanted to show his friend the real Jesus, not just the manger scene on display in front of the church.

"I have an idea," said the furry little rabbit. "Let's get back on the river."

So, the furry little rabbit and Rubber Duck slipped and slid down the river some more. The night grew darker and by the time they stopped again, the black sky was spotted with twinkling lights.

"Look there," the furry little rabbit pointed to the sky. "There's where you can see Jesus."

"Wow," said Rubber Duck. "How did those lights get way up there?"

The furry little rabbit let out a little laugh. "God put them there!"

"Just for Christmas?" Rubber Duck asked.

"No silly," said the furry little rabbit. "The stars are there every night…all year long."

"Wow," Rubber Duck said again, as he squinted towards the sky. "But I still don't see Jesus."

Again, the furry little rabbit thought hard. "Okay, follow me," he said at last.

Up, up, up a tall hill they climbed…and then down, down, down the tall hill they slid on their bottoms.

The two friends giggled and squealed all the way down, where they rolled and tumbled to a stop.

The furry little rabbit plucked his grinning face from the snow bank. "This is where I see Jesus," he announced.

Rubber Duck stuck his head in the snow bank. When he pulled his snow covered face out, he said, "I didn't see Jesus in there."

The furry little rabbit laughed and bounded off. Rubber Duck followed close.

When the furry little rabbit suddenly stopped near the edge of the forest, Rubber Duck nearly plowed him over.

"What's wrong?" Rubber Duck asked.

"Look," cried the furry little rabbit. "It's a baby bird, and it fell from that nest," he pointed high in the tree.

"Aw, it's shivering," said Rubber Duck. "Is it hurt?"

The furry little rabbit inched up close to the baby bird and hugged it with his blanket of fur. "There, there, little bird, it's okay," the furry little rabbit said. "Is that better?"

Instantly the little bird stopped shivering. Then it wiggled free and flew back to the nest.

"Amazing," said Rubber Duck. "I guess it was just cold and scared."

"Now, do you see Jesus?" the furry little rabbit asked.

"Um, no," Rubber Duck looked around. "Was he here? Did I miss him?"

The furry little rabbit buried his face in his hands, "No, no, no," he said. "This is so frustrating. I don't know how I can show you the real Jesus."

Rubber Duck hung his head. "I'm sorry," he said. "I've really been trying to see him."

Just then the furry little rabbit heard his mother calling. "Oh, that's Mama. I have to go home for dinner. Come with me," said the furry little rabbit.

"Are you sure your mama won't mind?" asked Rubber Duck.

"I'm sure," said the furry little rabbit. "Mama loves when I bring friends to visit."

"Alright then," said Rubber Duck, as he followed the furry little rabbit home.

Just as they reached the rabbit's burrow, the furry little rabbit and Rubber Duck saw some children decorating a snowman. They watched while the children draped popcorn on a string around the snowman's neck. A small boy stood on his tiptoes while he pushed a long, crooked carrot into the middle of the snowman's face. Another boy placed a red apple in each of the spots for eyes. A girl with rosy cheeks peeled the husk from an ear of corn. She pressed the silky husk on top of the head for hair, and the corn became the snowman's mouth. Finally, they watched as the children spread peanut butter all over a black hat and sprinkled it with cranberries and birdseed before they placed it on top of the snowman's head. At the snowman's feet, the children laid a sidewalk of sliced bread while they backed their way out of the woods.

"Another good Jesus sighting," said the furry little rabbit.

"Jesus is a snowman?" asked Rubber Duck.

"Oh, Rubber Duck! You are so silly. Jesus is not a snowman!" said the furry little rabbit, as he disappeared, head first, down a hole in the ground.

Rubber Duck hesitated beside the hole.

"Come on!" the furry little rabbit yelled. "It's okay!"

Rubber Duck looked left. Rubber Duck looked right. Then Rubber Duck jumped into the hole.

Now, it's a well known fact that furry little rabbits glide smoothly through the halls of their burrows, but rubber ducks on the other hand, bounce and land with a thump.

"Oh!" said Mama Rabbit. "Are you okay?"

"I…uh," Rubber Duck rubbed his head. "I think so."

"Oh dear," said Mama Rabbit. "You scraped your head. Come on, let me fix you up."

Rubber Duck slowly sat up so Mama Rabbit could bandage his head.

"How's that?" she asked, when she had finished.

"Better," said Rubber Duck. "Thank you."

The furry little rabbit let out a giggle. "You look silly Rubber Duck."

"You didn't warn me it would be a bumpy ride," said Rubber Duck.

"I forgot it was your first time," the furry little rabbit apologized.

"Would you like some carrot soup?" asked Mama Rabbit.

Rubber Duck didn't know if he liked carrot soup, but said he would love a bowl anyway.

"This is where I see Jesus," said the furry little rabbit, as he dipped his spoon into his bowl of hot soup.

Rubber Duck paused and looked into his bowl. "I don't see Jesus."

"He's not in the soup!" the furry little rabbit laughed so hard he almost fell off his chair.

"What's so funny?" asked Mama Rabbit.

"I've been trying all day to show Jesus to Rubber Duck," said the furry little rabbit.

"I've been trying real hard to see him too," said Rubber Duck, "but I keep missing him."

"Hmm," Mama Rabbit scrunched her face while she thought. "I think I know why you can't see Him," she said at last.

"You do?" asked Rubber Duck. "Why can't I see him?"

"Because you are looking with your eyes," decided Mama Rabbit.

Rubber Duck looked confused.

"If you truly want to see Jesus," Mama Rabbit looked him straight in the eyes. "You must look with your heart," she tapped him gently on the chest with one furry foot.

"How do I do that?" asked Rubber Duck.

"Close your eyes," Mama Rabbit instructed.

Rubber Duck closed his eyes.

"Now tell me what you two have done today," she said.

"Well…" said Rubber Duck, as he started to open his eyes.

"Keep your eyes closed," Mama Rabbit interrupted.

Rubber Duck snapped his eyes shut tight and began again.

"Well," he said, "First, we went sliding on the frozen river. Then we saw a manger scene of baby Jesus, but furry little rabbit said that wasn't the real Jesus.

Mama Rabbit lovingly patted the head of her little rabbit. "Go on," she said.

"Then we slid down a tall hill, and we stopped to help a baby bird that fell out of a nest," said Rubber Duck. "We saw some kids building a snowman with food for the animals. Then we came here, and you bandaged me up and fed us soup."

"I see," said Mama Rabbit. "And did any of those things make you feel all warm and fuzzy inside?" she asked.

Rubber Duck thought for a moment. "Yeah, it was fun slipping and sliding with my new friend, and helping that baby bird really warmed my heart," said Rubber Duck.

Mama Rabbit smiled.

"And," Rubber Duck added, "It felt pretty good when you fixed my head and gave me soup too."

"Jesus is love," said Mama Rabbit. "When people do good things and show love for each other, you can see Jesus is at work in their hearts."

"Mama takes good care of me," said the furry little rabbit. "It's easy to see Jesus at home, because Mama loves me so much."

Mama Rabbit smiled. "What's that I hear?" she asked, her ears pointed towards the opening of the burrow.

"Sounds like music," said the furry little rabbit. "Can we go see?"

"Sure," said Mama Rabbit, "but don't be gone long. It's getting late."

"Okay, Mama," said the furry little rabbit, as he and Rubber Duck darted out the opening.

The furry little rabbit and Rubber Duck followed the music until they reached the edge of the forest. Strolling down the street, paraded a group of children and adults. They carried lanterns and sang Christmas carols. Rubber Duck heard words like 'joy' and 'peace'.

"Come on," said the furry little rabbit when the group passed them by. "Let's follow them."

As they followed behind, Rubber Duck heard the carolers sing about a babe wrapped in swaddling clothing and lying in a manger. He heard them sing of a silent, holy night and he learned about how the wise men followed the star of Bethlehem to find Jesus, their newborn king. When the carolers stopped in front of a nursing home, one of the adults passed out trays of cookies for the carolers to take inside. As the doors to the home opened to welcome them inside, Rubber Duck heard the carolers singing at the top of their voices. He heard them sing '*Joy to the world, the Lord has come*'…and his heart felt warm.

Joy to the world, the Lord has come…

"Now, do you see Jesus?" asked the furry little rabbit, once the door had closed behind the last caroler.

"Yes," Rubber Duck smiled. "Now I see Jesus."

"Merry Christmas, Rubber Duck," said the furry little rabbit.

"Merry Christmas, furry little rabbit," said Rubber Duck. "Merry Christmas!"

We hope you have enjoyed 'Rubber Duck Finds Christmas'. If you would like to read other works by this author, look for 'Willow Crossing' (book 1) and 'Quest for the Glow' (book 2) of the 'Willow Crossing' series for middle graders. Coming soon…'Nameless Nickels' (book 3).

Also, coming soon… more Rubber Duck adventures!